THE CHIRP

RAJAT BANSAL

Published by InkQuills Publishing House
www.inkquills.in

First Edition 2021
All Rights Reserved. Copyright © 2021
ISBN: 978-93-90567-90-4

ACKNOWLEDGEMENT

I would like to thank my parents for supporting me in everything I wish to do, writing books being of them.

I feel extremely happy as my entire school know my parents by my name.

Contents

Chapter 1 - THE CHIRP 1

Chapter 2 - MY VISIT TO THE VILLAGE 6

Chapter 3 - THOSE LOVELY 5 MINUTES... 11

Chapter 4 - MOTHER'S DAY 15

Chapter 5 - THE SCARY NIGHT 20

Chapter 6 - MY LAST DAY AT SCHOOL..... 25

Chapter 7 - JEALOUS FRUITS 29

Chapter 8 - THE UNGRATEFUL KID 33

Chapter 9 - POWER OF FAITH 37

Chapter 10 - THE LIAR 42

Chapter 1
THE CHIRP

I never had pets. Somehow, I disliked the idea of taking care of them all the time. Their food, walks, cries, and howling could be a mess in my peaceful home.

Diwali was approaching and my neighbours knocked on the door. I thought uncle and aunt must have come to wish Diwali before leaving for my hometown. But it was none of them. It was their son with a pair of birds in a cage that was dangling from his hand. He looked at me with a smile. I gave them a puzzled look.

He then spoke,

"May I come in and keep it down? My hands are hurting."

Still puzzled, I made way for him to enter. The birds were continuously chirping. They were so beautiful that. I could not take my eyes off them. However, I was still waiting for him to speak further.

"We all are leaving for our home town for Diwali but cannot carry the birds along. So, my mother asked me to hand them to you for a few days if you don't have any issues."

I frowned.

Umm! Let me ask my mother.

I got up and went to another room. I was alone. It was me who was buying time to think about the birds.

I came back.

'OK. My mother has agreed to keep them. So, for how many days are you going?'

'A week.'

I looked at the small cage again. He had already kept the food for the next day in the cage so I had no burden on me for a day at least.

He left and I, without any interest, kept the cage in the veranda and started scrolling my phone.

Almost 5 hours had passed since he left the birds at my place and they were still chirping.

These birds keep chirping the whole day. They don't let me study. I don't know why I agreed to keep these.

The day soon ended with me staring at the cage.

In the morning, my mother returned home. She was in the sitting room when she heard loud chirps. She was amazed to see the cute birds.

She came to my room while I was fast asleep and shook me.

'Hey! Wake up, Vivek.'

"What happened, mum?"

'Where did these birds come from?'

'Oh! Those little monsters! Our neighbour's child dropped them yes as they were going out and they could not take care of them.'

I continued, 'I don't like them. They are so disturbing, I feel uncomfortable.'

She didn't speak a word. She went closer to them and started speaking,

'Hey, beautiful ladies. How are you? I have never seen something as beautiful as you.'

The birds chirped a little louder.

'MUM! Is it only me or you too feel that they are answering you?'

'These creatures do respond to us, son. You just need to love them'.

I went closer to them. For the first time, I admired their beauty and started talking to them.

Chapter 2
MY VISIT TO THE VILLAGE

My holidays were about to start. I was convincing my father for a holiday to a hill station as I love to play with snow. I always wait for snowfalls. But my father had different plans.

'This time I will take you to a new place.'

'Oh wow! A new place? Um! Manali? Shimla?'

'No. Guess a little more. A new place'

'Mum! Any idea?'

She does not respond. Just smiles.

'Dad, tell me, please. Where are we going this time? You are spoiling all the excitement.'

He hangs his head in sadness.

'OK So… The surprise is that we are going to our village, my ancestral place.'

'What? A village? No! A big NO!'

But it has been finalised that this time the vacations would be in their ancestral village.

The next day, they all started the early morning by car. Amol was upset so he closed his eyes and acted asleep. A few hours had passed when the AC of the car was turned off and the mirrors were lowered. A cool soothing breeze hit Amol.

He woke up rubbing his eyes just to see scenic beauty.

'Wow! Where are we? What is this place? Are we not going to the village?'

His parents looked at each other and smiled.

His mother looked at him and said, 'Um! Why are you asking so?'

'I am feeling really good. The view is so beautiful and clean. I can feel the fresh air. I feel we are heading towards a beautiful place. Tell me, please. Where are we going?'

'We are moving close to our village.'

'What? Really?'

Amol was ready to ask a few more questions when he saw a dancing peacock.

'Oh wow! What a sight! I have never seen a dancing peacock in my life. It is so beautiful.'

His eyes widened with joy. Rubbing his eyes even harder, he now sat closer to the window to enjoy the scenic beauty.

As they headed towards the village, he started enjoying it even more. The cool breeze, the animals and most importantly the farms. He urged me to stop the car to get the feel of the paddy there.

As they stopped, Amol ran towards the handpump, looking at it in astonishment.

'Dad, what is this?

'Come, I will show you.'

Excitedly, they went closer to it.

As Amol's dad started moving the handle, the water started gushing down.

Amol jumped in shock.

'Wow! Water! Is this a water machine? We have taps at our homes. They look so boring. This is exciting.'

His dad started laughing. Like an enthusiastic child, Amol started running around in the village, exploring and discovering new things.

He started enjoying every inch of the village.

Chapter 3
THOSE LOVELY
5 MINUTES

It was mid-July and the rainy season was about to approach.

We stayed on the ground floor and there was a huge playground in front of our building. We all played there after school and had a lot of fun. There were a lot of pets in our society, most of them were dogs. I too loved dogs but my mother somehow disliked them.

That day, the sky was black and it was about to rain heavily. All my friends and I were playing after school. It had started drizzling and we were in no mood to return home. We were excited.

My mother too came looking for me. Since it was only drizzling till then, she was not much worried.

Soon there was lightning and a thunderstorm. It started raining heavily. There was a power cut in the entire area. Soon it got dark, extremely dark all around.

I was rushing home when I heard a feeble cry of a puppy. It was dark and there was water all around. Following the cry, I went to the place and saw a small white puppy crying. It was very cute. I wanted to hold it into my arms but I feared my mother's scolding. However, at last, I did pick it up.

By then my mother had come down searching for me. She had a torch in her hand and was looking for me throwing light everywhere.

'Adi! Adi!'

I heard her but I was in no mood to get noticed by her. She called my name and went back. I decided to take care of the puppy.

My mother came back calling out my name.

'Ma! I am here. Just 5 minutes and I am coming back to you.'

'But what are you doing there? I have been looking for you.'

I didn't reply.

As she came closer to me, she saw that I had arranged a warm bed for the pup to save it from the heavy rainfall.

She had tears in her eyes. Tears of love and joy!

Chapter 4
MOTHER'S DAY

Tomorrow is the Mother's Day.

Father and I have decided on a gift and few other things for mum but we will have to try to act normal. She doesn't know my father's involvement in this.

It's 11:30 now and my father and I are waiting for the clock to strike 12 am. As soon as it does, we will keep a card below her pillow, and in the morning, we will gift her a fabulous costume.

Shh…! It's 12 am and we both are keeping the card beneath her pillow. I hope she doesn't wake up.

'Ah! Job done!' My father and I said unanimously.

Now, let's wait for the morning.

It's 7'o o'clock and I have just woken up. Let's try to act normal and act as if we don't know anything about today's event.

'By the way, I can't see Dad. Where has he gone? I hope not to his friends today.'

I said to myself.

My mother is working in the kitchen. Let's go and ask for milk. I will try best to obey her and not give her any chance to doubt me.

Oh! She's going to the bedroom to clean it. I should go to the bedroom and sit on that pillow so that she doesn't clean that area.

'Phew! We are safe.'

Now I think I can ask her about the father.

'Mum, where's Dad?'

'He has gone to the market to get milk. It's pretty late though.'

Ding … Ding!

'Oh! It's your father,' mother said.

'Dad, where were you?'

'Will tell you later.'

It's afternoon now and this is the time my mother sleeps, basically, the best time for us to decorate the house. But we don't have the materials.

Hey! The mystery and the problem both solved. The father just came out of his room with the items for decoration. He had gone to the market to bring milk and decoration items.

Thank goodness! We have completed the decoration on time. My mother is still sleeping. I should take out the card and keep it on the centre table.

But no!

There's someone at the door … A delivery boy with a big colourful box.

My father just revealed that it's his arrangement.

'It's a cake.'

I am so happy and shocked at the same time.

Everything is set. Now, it's time to act sleeping!

It's 4 pm and mother is in the sitting room.

'What's there?'

'HAPPY MOTHER'S DAY!' we said aloud from behind as mother was looking at the gift.

My mum's eyes are teary.

'It's one of my best days. Thank you so much for arranging all this.'

It seems like a big success. Father and I are so happy.

Chapter 5
THE SCARY NIGHT

I always wanted to watch horror movies because my parents always asked me otherwise. I always had that curiosity to do what I was told not to do.

So, it was a weekend and I heard my parents that they were going to watch a horror movie when I was asleep. I was excited and sad at the same time. I so badly wanted to watch it but my parents in no way were going to allow me.

We all finished dinner half an hour earlier that day and they asked me to go to bed saying they wanted to discuss something important. But I knew; there was a movie plan.

I went to their room and pretended to fall asleep there only, thinking if they let me be there, I would be able to watch the movie secretly.

But no. My mother pulled me out of the bed and literally pushed me towards my room.

I headed towards it in disagreement.

I wanted to watch the movie anyway. I kept peeping from my room to get an opportunity of slipping into their room.

Just after a few minutes, my mother got up to take water and I quietly entered the room and hid under the bed.

I was watching from under the bed and was super proud of my achievement of barging into my parents' room to fulfil my desire.

Only a few minutes had passed when a scary scene came and I screamed from under the bed. My parents were shocked to see me there. I got a little scolding out of care and was sent back to my room.

I understood that watching a horror movie is not my cup of tea.

I just tried sleeping with the lights on. I covered my face too. Whenever I am scared, I play songs on my tab. But that day the tab was also not there.

Suddenly I heard my favourite playlist being played in the reverse order.

After a few minutes, my room's light also started flickering.

I got scared and shut my eyes tight. The light got stable soon. I was trying to calm myself when suddenly I saw a shadow with horns behind the curtains.

I screamed and started howling in fear.

Seeing me in such a state, my parents came out from behind the curtains and hugged me.

I was shocked to see them there and soon understood their plan.

It was all staged to make me understand that watching horror movies at my age is not a good idea at all.

Their plan worked very well, indeed!

Chapter 6
MY LAST DAY AT SCHOOL

I always disliked school. I mean who likes to wear the same dress every day and eat the same kind of food. The subjects were so boring that I never developed an interest in studies. The teachers were really sweet and hard-working but extremely strict at the same time. The walls were grey and so boring. The only things that occupied the space were the frames of freedom fighters whose names I didn't even know.

The chalk and the duster were the saddest part of the entire day. They jointly bored us. I always looked forward to going back home as soon as possible and having good warm food. I only enjoyed the bus ride with all my friends. The best part was jumping in the bus whenever it crossed a speed-breaker.

I wanted to pass school as soon as possible and get admission to a college as I had heard that college is the best place to enjoy life.

But today when it is the last day of my school, my eyes are full of tears. Never thought that the real last day of my school will be a terrible day. My heart was heavy seeing people hugging each other, signing scrap books, and writing parting notes on school shirts.

I was looking for my gang. We have been best friends since childhood. I was not ready to be separated from them. Then I saw them coming towards me running from the football ground. They kicked the ball towards me and I missed it as my eyes were full of tears imagining them being away from me.

As they came and hugged me tight, we all burst into tears. We all went to our classroom and picked up the duster and a few chalks as memory. This was the most hated pair back then we all left notes on the blackboard of our classes for our teachers. A few loving notes for the teachers who gave the best years of our lives.

We all went towards the canteen and hugged all the boys who served us all these years. They had tears too.

We were about to leave when the peon came running towards us. He handed over all the balls that he had collected when we broke the rules of cricket.

Before leaving the school and exchanging phone numbers, we all went to our principal's room to say a final good bye and take her blessings.

Chapter 7
JEALOUS FRUITS

It was probably one of the hottest days of summer when my mother and I went out to buy some juicy fruits. I was craving some juicy mangoes. Even the thought of them was making my mouth water.

Soon we came back home and kept all the fruits on the table. All the fruits were fresh but I wanted to eat only mangoes.

It was evening when my mother called me to have some fruits.

'Come, Arjun, let us have some fruits. I have cut fruits for you.'

'I want to have only mangoes. They are the best.'

'That is not right. You should have all of them.'

'No, please. I don't want to eat any other fruit. I only like mangoes.'

My mother insisted on eating other fruits as well, but I didn't.

At night when I woke up to have water, I was surprised to see the other fruits fighting. I was shocked to realise that I could hear them. I hid behind the refrigerator and tried listening to them.

'This giant fruit, the so-called king of fruits, huh, must be very proud. Everyone wants to eat it only as if it has no taste and benefits. I hate mangoes, said the apple.

'Same here. Like, look at me. I am so beautiful and juicy but this boy doesn't want to have me,' said the strawberry.

They all started fighting and protesting against the mango. The mango was quiet and did not respond.

In the morning, we were busy with our routine when I went to the sitting room looking for my laptop and saw that all the fruits, except mango, were rotten. Then I had a sudden flashback to what happened last night. Probably that was the reason behind their state. I decided that I will eat all kinds of fruits from today so that none of them is sad.

It was evening. My mother started cutting fruits and called me.

I stopped her and asked, 'Why are you cutting only mangoes?'

She replied, 'Because you like them and don't eat any other fruit.'

I said, 'OH, that was yesterday. Today cut all the fruits but in small quantities, so I can eat and enjoy the taste of all fruits.'

Soon he started eating all fruits and all of the fruits now were happy and not jealous.

Chapter 8
THE UNGRATEFUL KID

Once upon a time, there lived a father and a son. The kid was a pampered child and didn't value his father's hard- earned money. Every day he demanded new costly things.

'Dad, I want a new car.'

'Another car? We already have 5 of them!'

'But all are outdated now. I don't like any.'

'But the latest one is only a few months old. You haven't driven it yet.'

'I just want it, Dad! You are getting me a new car or not?'

Arjun actually shouted at his father.

'I cannot give you whatever you ask for! You have to set limits.'

'But we have a lot of money. We can easily get a new car.'

'It is my hard-earned money. I cannot let you waste it. You need to understand it.'

Arjun left the room in anger banging the door. His father tried a lot to make him understand but the young man didn't listen.

He didn't eat for a day and didn't talk to his father. His father got worried about him and went to talk to him.

After a long conversation, both agreed on the condition that the day the young man is successful at earning any amount of money, he will get what he wants from the amount earned.

The young man jumped in excitement thinking earning money isn't a tough job at all. He went out and his father wished him the best of his luck. The entire day passed and the young man returned home tired and exhausted.

'Oh, so you are home? Wow! Give me the money you have earned today. Show me, show me. It must be a lot of money,' the father said, extending his hand towards his son.

Arjun hung his head in shame and took out a few notes. They were a small bunch of only 50 notes, divided into smaller denominations.

'It is okay, son. Come on, let us go and spend this money on buying whatever you want.'

The smart father deliberately said such to test his son and there happened exactly that what had expected.

'No, Dad. This is my hard-earned money and I don't want to spend it on buying non-essential things.'

The young man learnt the lesson the hard way.

Chapter 9
POWER OF FAITH

Ananya was an eight-year-old girl. She was a good child and had absolute faith in God. However, she was very stubborn. Most of the time, she did what she wanted. She thought she was a big girl and could handle everything by herself.

Her parents remained worried for her but she would rarely listen to them. They tried to explain a lot of things to her but then left a few things to be understood with time.

She loved cricket so they put her into practice, thinking sports might bring discipline to her life.

One day, her mother got late for picking up from her academy. She informed her that she would be late and Ananya needs to wait at reception only.

After waiting for about half an hour, she began to feel restless.

She called her mother and informed her that she was leaving for home on her own.

'No, please. Listen to me. Don't come alone, I will be there soon, said the mother.

'Mumma, I am hungry. I want to eat something. I am coming, don't worry.'

'Ananya, listen to me, doll. The area is not safe for kids. Also, the sun is setting and, it is getting darker.'

Ananya hung up the phone. She wanted to reach home as soon as possible. Thus, she started walking towards home. She kept on walking fearlessly until she entered one wrong road. Initially, she had failed to make out that it was a wrong turn, but when she didn't see the park, which was a landmark for her home, she realised that she was lost. But being a stubborn child, she continued walking.

When she looked at her watch and realised that 10 extra minutes had already passed, she got a little scared.

She closed her eyes and remembered God.

'I am sorry, God. I should have listened to my mother. Please help me,' she said with tears in her eyes and kept on walking.

Soon she realised that a young boy with a sack in his hand was following her.

Ananya had heard stories about young children being abducted. She got even more scared now.

Nevertheless, she continued walking and apologising to god for her mistake. She was very tired by now but she did not stop to avoid the boy following her.

When she looked around, she realised that she was very near to her society. However, she was unable to find the right path.

She prayed again, 'God, please help me. I know you are near. You have shown me the right path, please help me a little more.'

She had just completed saying this when she heard a lady say, 'Ananya, what are you doing in another lane? Come here and play with kids here.'

Ananya took a sigh of relief and ran towards her home. The young boy had disappeared.

Ananya reached home safely and hugged her mother tight.

Chapter 10
THE LIAR

Once upon a time, there was a kid who lied a lot to his parents. His parents were worried about him a lot fearing he might get into trouble someday, but he would never listen.

One day, he broke the shower but didn't tell his parents, instead fixed it the way he could.

When his mother went to have a shower, it fell on her and she got hurt.

The parents asked the kid if he broke it. But the child refused. This was his regular affair.

Another day, he left his bat on the ground and returned home. Upon asking he said that his friend had taken it. At night when his father returned home with his bat, he asked where he had left it. The child started making excuses. But the parents understood that he was lying again.

They thought of teaching him a lesson.

One day, when he returned home after playing, he saw his robot broken.

'Oh No! Who broke this? Mum, do you know anything about it?'

'No. I have no idea. I remain in the kitchen most of the time.'

He began waiting desperately for his father to return from the office to ask him about the broken robot.

However, when he asked his father about the robot, his father also denied having any information about it.

The young boy was trying to join the pieces of the robot but was failing.

'Had I known who broke it and how, I could have fixed it.'

He was howling in anger.

When his parents saw him in such a state, they came up to him and the father admitted his mistake.

'Dad, had you told me, I could have fixed it. Why did you lie to me?'

'I felt lying is a good thing because you keep on doing it.'

The young boy understood his mistake and apologised to his father.

'Nobody is perfect. We all make mistakes, do blunders but lying is not the right thing. To accept mistakes and say sorry is.'

By then, the mother had joined the parts of the robot.

The parents had finally taught him a lesson.